My Dinosaur Adventure

a personalized storybook

Illustrated by
Valarie Webb

Printed in the USA
Hefty Publishing Company
Patented
U.S. Patent Number 5,114,291
www.hefty.com

1

My Dinosaur Adventure
was created especially for

Ryan Tata
at the age of 4

With all our love,
Ms. Jackson, Ms. Ginger,
Mrs. Jantz and M Bev
June 24, 2003

3

Ryan Tata of St. Albert, Alberta had a special dream. His favorite books to read from the library were always those about dinosaurs, but he wanted to learn a lot more about them. As he was thinking about this, a beautiful white unicorn appeared at his bedroom window.

5

To his surprise, the unicorn spoke, "Ryan, I want to take you to the Land of the Dinosaurs. Can you come with me?"

Ryan said, "Wow! I would love to go, but first I must ask permission and leave a note for Garnet, Kent and Hailey." Moments later, the unicorn whisked him back in time to the Land of the Dinosaurs.

When Ryan and the unicorn arrived at the shore of the beautiful lake, an apotosaurus (uh-pat-o-SORE-us) greeted them. He was longer than a big school bus.

"What's your name?" asked Ryan.

"I don't have one," answered the plant-eating dinosaur sadly. "No one has ever named any of us."

Ryan thought for a while and then said, "I will call you Stretch."

"Look at that mountain over there!" shouted Ryan, pointing off into the distance. "Is it on fire?" he asked.

"Oh no, that's just a volcano," replied the unicorn. "Look all around you. The Land of the Dinosaurs is filled with many, many volcanoes, swamps and fern jungles."

Ryan added, "It's also very hot!"

While exploring, they met a stegosaurus (steg-uh-SORE-us). "He sure does have a lot of sharp points on his back," whispered Ryan.

"Those are called plates," said the unicorn. "A stegosaurus uses them for protection. They also trap heat from the sun to help keep them warm."

Ryan told the stegosaurus, "A great name for you would be Spike."

13

14

Next, Ryan and the unicorn entered a dense, humid forest where they found giant ferns and many reptiles of all sizes and shapes. While there, they heard a strange, snapping sound in the distance and cautiously crept closer to investigate. After all, Ryan had wanted to come here to learn as much as he could about dinosaurs!

Not far away, they met an allosaurus (al-us-SORE-us). She had large teeth and stood on powerful, hind legs. A huge tail helped her to stand up.

"So you are the one who is making all that noise," said Ryan. "I shall name you Alli."

Alli said, "Thank you," as she handed Ryan a branch of flowers.

18

Ryan was having so much fun in the Land of the Dinosaurs that he had not noticed that his friend the unicorn was crying. "Why are you crying?" asked Ryan.

"You have given names to everyone today except me," sighed the unicorn.

"Oh, I'm sorry. Ariel would be the perfect name for you," said Ryan.

"I love it!" smiled the wide-eyed unicorn with a big grin. "Thank you!"

As they were talking, a tiny compsognathus (komp-sog-NAY-thus), about the size of a cat, raced past them and said, "You must follow me. There is something you will want to see." Ryan and Ariel chased after him.

"Wow! He is as fast as lightning. That's a great name for him," shouted Ryan as he ran.

They ran and ran until they came to some rugged, rocky cliffs. Lightning showed Ryan a nest along the top of one of the cliffs and directed him to get a close look. The nest contained three baby pterodactyls (ter-uh-DAK-tuls).

"Who is supposed to be taking care of these babies?" asked Ryan.

"I am!" echoed a voice, circling above them. Just then a large pterodactyl glided past them. Ryan found it hard to believe that a lizard could fly. Its wing span was about as long as his arm. Ryan decided that Dack would be a fine name for a flying lizard. The father pterodactyl glided down to the nest. Ariel was quietly talking to Dack, but Ryan could not hear what they were saying.

Ryan, Ariel and the pterodactyl flew back across the Land of the Dinosaurs until they once more reached the beautiful lake. This time Ryan saw a lot of activity at the water's edge. Dinosaurs were decorating the beach with streamers and balloons. Ryan wanted to help decorate and wondered if he could go to the party.

As they landed, a pentaceratops (pen-tuh-SARE-uh-tops) rushed to greet them. Ryan quickly counted the five horns on his head and decided to call him Penti. Then he asked if he could help them decorate.

"I want you to come with me, but for a different reason," replied Penti. "We have a surprise for you!"

The dinosaurs were gathered around a large two-tiered cake. "What a beautiful cake!" exclaimed Ryan.

"It's for you!" shouted his new friends. Now Ryan knew what Ariel had whispered to Dack. The dinosaurs realized that Ryan had to return soon and had wanted to help him remember his first visit to the Land of the Dinosaurs.

After the party, Alli, the allosaurus, told Ryan that it was time to leave for St. Albert, Alberta. Ryan was a bit sad, but could hardly wait to tell Garnet, Kent and Hailey about his exciting adventures. Before he left, they all thanked Ryan for the nice names he had given them.

Ariel flew Ryan home and said, "I also have a surprise for you, Ryan." In his room, he found a dinosaur cake with a personalized card signed by all the dinosaurs. Ryan hugged Ariel for making his secret dream come true and told her how much he had enjoyed his trip to the Land of the Dinosaurs. "I will never forget what you have done for me! Thank you for my fabulous dinosaur adventure."

Here are the pronunciations for
the dinosaurs you have read
about in MY DINOSAUR
ADVENTURE. Use your book to
spell them correctly.

(uh - pat - o - SORE - us)
(steg-uh-SORE-us)
(al-uh-SORE-us)
(komp-sog-NAY-thus)
(ter-uh-DAK-tuls)
(pen-tuh-SARE-uh-tops)

What other dinosaurs can you
name, Ryan?

Create-A-Book byglenn
http://www.create-a-book.ab.ca
81 Forest Grove
St. Albert, Alberta, Canada, T8N 2Y1
Phone: 780-460-1938
Fax: 780-419-2106
Glenn@ecn.ab.ca